ORLAND PARK PUBLIC LIBRARY

P9-DDL-306

NOV   2000

DISCARD

ORLAND PARK PUBLIC LIBRARY
AILEEN S. ANDREW MEMORIAL
14760 PARK LANE
ORLAND PARK, ILLINOIS 60
349-8138

DEMCO

The Wisdom Bird

ORLAND PARK PUBLIC LIBRARY

The Wisdom Bird
A Tale of Solomon and Sheba

Retold by Sheldon Oberman • Illustrated by Neil Waldman

Boyds Mills Press

ORLAND PARK PUBLIC LIBRARY

Text copyright © 2000 by Sheldon Oberman
Illustrations copyright © 2000 by Neil Waldman
All rights reserved

Published by Caroline House
Boyds Mills Press, Inc.
A Highlights Company
815 Church Street
Honesdale, Pennsylvania 18431
Printed in Hong Kong

Publisher Cataloging-in-Publication Data

Oberman, Sheldon.
   The wisdom bird: a tale of Solomon and Sheba / by Sheldon
Oberman ; Illustrated by Neil Waldman.—1st ed.
[32]p. : col. ill. ;   cm.
Summary: King Solomon learns a lesson from a little bird in this story
based on Jewish and African tales.
ISBN 1-56397-816-4
1. Solomon, King of Israel—Juvenile fiction. 2. Sheba, Queen of—
Juvenile fiction. [1. Solomon, King of Israel—Fiction. 2. Sheba,
Queen of—Fiction.] I. Waldman, Neil, ill. II. Title.
   [E]—dc21 2000 AC   CIP
 99-63098

First edition, 2000
The text of this book is set in 16-point Usherwood Book.
The illustrations are done in acrylic.

Visit us on the World Wide Web at www.boydsmillspress.com

10 9 8 7 6 5 4 3 2 1

For Howard Schwartz and Barbara Rush
—S. O.

For Maurice Meyer, the most wonderful uncle
—N. W.

KING SOLOMON could answer any question. He could solve any problem.

Even the birds talked about his wisdom. They flew all the way to Africa, telling everyone, "King Solomon is the wisest man in the world!"

They even told the Queen of Sheba, who was also very wise. Some say she was the wisest woman in the world.

When the queen heard about King Solomon, she said, "I want to meet this clever man." She called together her servants, her warriors, and her nobles. She told them, "We are going to Jerusalem."

They sailed by ship across the Red Sea, then they traveled by camel caravan through the Negev Desert. Finally, they reached the high gates of Jerusalem.

Her servants sang and drummed. Her warriors danced and shook their spears. Her nobles brought forward gifts of gold and silver, spices and incense, and the many wonderful creatures of Africa, but the gates stayed shut.

Finally, the queen called out, "I am the Queen of Sheba. I have come to meet King Solomon!"

For a moment, everything was still and silent. Then, from inside the city, a hundred trumpets blew, the high gates of Jerusalem opened wide, and out came Solomon.

"Great queen," he said, "you have traveled so far and you have brought me so much. What can I give you in return?"

"Teach me something important," she replied, "something worth all these gifts and all my time and trouble."

King Solomon invited her to sit beside his throne. She watched as he solved every problem that his people brought him. She listened as he read to her from his book, *The Song of Songs*. She asked him many questions, and he answered every one.

"Now," said Solomon, "have I taught you something worth all your gifts and all your time and trouble?"

She shook her head. "No," she said. "You have great knowledge, but show me what you can do with it."

"Name anything," said Solomon. "If it can be done, I promise I will do it."

"Build a palace out of bird beaks," she said.

Everyone was shocked. That would take all the beaks of all the birds of the world.

"I have promised," said Solomon, "so I must do it." He led her to the top of the highest tower in the city. He called out to the birds of the north and the south, the east and the west. "Come to Jerusalem. Give up your beaks to me."

Hour after hour, the sky grew darker and darker with beating wings. It grew louder and louder with chirps and caws, hoots and trills, until all the birds of the world had arrived, except for one—the hoopoe, a small colorful bird with a long, thin beak.

"It has disobeyed me," said Solomon, and he called to the eagles and owls, the falcons and hawks. "Search for the hoopoe. Find the hoopoe. Bring the hoopoe here!"

They searched and found the hoopoe bird and quickly brought it back. The little bird begged Solomon, "Please do not punish me. I was on my way, but I stopped to find you a gift. I've found three gifts, three things you do not know."

"King Solomon knows everything!" the other birds called out. "How can a bird know more than the wisest king!"

"Little hoopoe," said Solomon, "if you can teach me one thing I do not know, I will set you free."

So the hoopoe asked Solomon three questions.

"Here is my first question," said the hoopoe. "What was made the longest time ago and meant to last the longest time from now?"

Solomon answered easily. "It is the world and all its creatures. You birds were made at the beginning of time and meant to last till the end of time." He asked the birds, "Am I right?"

They all agreed: the geese and ducks, the swans and pelicans, the cormorants and cranes. "Oh yes, oh yes," they said.

Solomon thought, *The birds are meant to last forever, but I am changing them.*

"Here is my second question," said the hoopoe. "What is so gentle it is used to feed a baby, yet so strong it is used to break through earth and wood, to build a home, and to fight off enemies?"

Solomon answered easily. "A bird's beak. Birds use their beaks to gently feed their young. Yet they also use their beaks to dig through earth and trees for food, to build their nests, and to protect their families." Solomon asked the birds, "Am I right?"

All the birds agreed: the parrots and woodpeckers, the crows and kingfishers, the hummingbirds and jays. "Oh yes, oh yes," they said and sadly lowered their beaks.

Solomon thought, *Their beaks are so important. What will they do without them*?

"Here is my third question," said the hoopoe. "What drop of water does not rise from the ground or fall from the sky?"

Again Solomon knew the answer. "A tear. It rises from an unhappy heart. It falls from a sad eye." He asked the birds, "Am I right?"

Again they all agreed: the mourning doves and meadowlarks, the nightingales and chickadees, the peacocks and parakeets. "Oh yes, oh yes," they said, and their tears began to flow.

Solomon thought, *The birds are crying because I am taking away their beaks*. He felt so sad for them that a tear came to his eye.

CEDAR PARK PUBLIC LIBRARY

313 6723

ORLAND PARK PUBLIC LIBRARY

"Great king," said the hoopoe bird, "you have answered all my questions. I have failed."

King Solomon lifted the hoopoe onto his finger. "Little bird, you did not fail," he said. "I knew the answers, but I did not understand what the answers meant. Now I do."

Solomon called to all the birds. "Now I understand that you are important and your beaks are important, and your tears are important. I will not hurt you or any creature just to show my power. I will not punish this bird of wisdom, and I will not take your beaks."

What a celebration! Those millions of birds rose into the sky, soaring and swooping and calling out the happy news. Yet just as quickly they returned and settled into silence, for Solomon had turned to Sheba.

"Great queen," said Solomon, "I promised to build a palace of bird beaks. I have failed."

The queen smiled. "You did not fail," she said. "I wanted you to teach me something important, and you did. You taught me that it is better to break a promise than to do something that is wrong."

"Will you free me from my promise?" asked Solomon.

The queen shook her head. "Not yet," she said.

"Then what do you want me to do?" he asked.

"Think of a way to reward the hoopoe bird," she said, "for it has taught a king and queen, and it has saved all the birds of the world."